Around the Table That Grandad Built

Melanie Heuiser Hill   illustrated by Jaime Kim

WALKER BOOKS
AND SUBSIDIARIES

LONDON · BOSTON · SYDNEY · AUCKLAND

This is the table that Grandad built.

These are the sunflowers picked by my cousins
Set on the table that Grandad built.

These are the napkins sewn by Mum

Surrounding the sunflowers picked by my cousins
Set on the table that Grandad built.

These are our plates – red, orange and yellow ...

That go with the napkins sewn by Mum
Surrounding the sunflowers picked by my cousins
Set on the table that Grandad built.

These are the glasses
from Mum and Dad's wedding ...

Set by our plates – red, orange and yellow –
That go with the napkins sewn by Mum
Surrounding the sunflowers picked by my cousins
Set on the table that Grandad built.

These are the forks and spoons and knives –
gifts from Dad's grandma long ago ...

Placed by the glasses from Mum and Dad's wedding
Set by our plates – red, orange and yellow –

That go with the napkins sewn by Mum
Surrounding the sunflowers picked by my cousins
Set on the table that Grandad built.

This is the squash that took over our garden.
These are the potatoes and peppers we roasted.
And these are the beans, overflowing the bowl!

This is the stack of toasty tamales.
These are the samosas, spicy and hot.
And this is the rice pudding we have every year.

This is the bread – still warm! – that Gran baked.
This is the butter made by us kids.
And this is Dad's huckleberry jam –
 mmmMMMMMM.

And *here* are the pies! I made this one myself!

For these hands we hold,
for tasty good food,
for family and friends,

for grace that is given
and love that is shared,

we give thanks ...

around this table that Grandad built.

For Mom and Dad, who bake and build
and gather us around the table
M. H. H.

For my family
J. K.

First published 2019 by Walker Books Ltd
87 Vauxhall Walk, London SE11 5HJ

2 4 6 8 10 9 7 5 3 1

Text © 2019 Melanie Heuiser Hill
Illustrations © 2019 Jaime Kim

The right of Melanie Heuiser Hill and Jaime Kim to be identified as the author and illustrator of this
work has been asserted by them in accordance with the Copyright, Designs and Patents Act 1988

This book has been typeset in Youbee Bold

Printed in China

British Library Cataloguing in Publication Data:
a catalogue record for this book is available from the British Library

ISBN 978-1-4063-8878-7

www.walker.co.uk